# STEEDS OF THE GODS

Lucy Coats is the author of more than thirty books for readers of all ages, including *Atticus the Storyteller's 100 Greek Myths*, which was shortlisted for the Blue Peter Book Award. She began her storytelling career as a bookseller, editor and journalist, and has been fascinated by myths and legends ever since she can remember. She lives in deepest south Northamptonshire with her husband and three unruly dogs. When she is not writing, she cooks, grows vegetables and sits in her stone circle, looking at the stars.

Beasts of Olympus:

BEAST KEEPER
HOUND OF HADES
STEEDS OF THE GODS
DRAGON HEALER

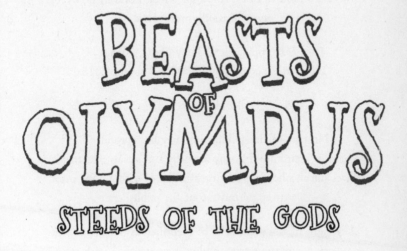

# BEASTS OF OLYMPUS

## STEEDS OF THE GODS

## LUCY COATS

with illustrations by
David Roberts

Piccadilly
PRESS

First published in Great Britain in 2015
by Piccadilly Press
Northburgh House, 10 Northburgh Street, London EC1V 0AT
www.piccadillypress.co.uk

Text copyright © Lucy Coats, 2015
Illustrations copyright © David Roberts, 2015

A CIP catalogue record for this book is available from
the British Library

ISBN: 978–1–84812–452–3

1 3 5 7 9 10 8 6 4 2

Typeset by Palimpsest Book Production Limited,
Falkirk, Stirlingshire
Printed in the UK by Clays Ltd, St Ives plc

Piccadilly Press is an imprint of the Bonnier Publishing Group
www.bonnierpublishing.com

For Faith Jackson, who reads enough books
to feed a Griffin

# 1
# THE GOD FROM THE SEA

The first Demon knew of his latest Important Visitor was when he heard Melanie the naiad shriek. He dropped his shovel in the poo-barrow and rushed over to the spring outside the Stables of the Gods to see what was happening. Melanie stood shivering and curtsying at the side of her spring, her long blue hair streaming down her back. In the middle of the water stood a huge black-bearded figure, wearing a crown of jewelled seashells. He held a large golden trident in his left hand.

'Pah!' he spat, wringing out his cloak and robes and striding up to Demon. 'Fresh water. Mimsy-flimsy stuff. Give me a pool of salty sea brine any day.'

Demon's heart sank into his sandals as he bowed low. An early morning visit from a god was never good news – and this was Zeus's own brother. What could Poseidon, god of the sea, want with him at this hour?

'How can I help you, Your Watery Wondrousness?' he asked, looking worriedly at poor Melanie, who had dived back into her spring, obviously horrified by the messy silvery seaweed now decorating its surface but not daring to say so.

'Ha!' said Poseidon, clapping Demon on the shoulder so hard he fell on his backside in the dust. 'Watery Wondrousness. I like it. Up you get now, stable boy, I need to talk to you.' He reached down and offered a hand wearing an assortment of rings which seemed to be set with sapphires the size and shape of barnacles. Demon took it gingerly. It felt cold and rather wet, and the jewel 'barnacles' scraped his fingers rather, but he didn't say anything. It was best not to with gods. They took offence very easily, he'd found, and that could lead to Bad Things.

Poseidon was looking about him. The nine green heads of Doris the Hydra were peering shyly round the doors of the stables, long eyelashes fluttering. Demon could see Arnie the griffin lurking about behind Doris.

'That the beastie you cured for Hera?' the god asked. 'Looks pretty healthy to me.'

'Yes, Your Serene Saltiness,' said Demon. 'It helps me out round the stables now.' Doris fluttered its twenty-seven pairs of eyelashes and rattled its buckets.

'Snackies?' it asked hopefully, drool running down its chins and plopping onto the floor. Demon ignored it. He'd only just cured its bellyache from eating too much ambrosia cake and he wasn't risking a repeat.

'Show me around, stable boy,' said Poseidon,

dropping his rather seaweedy arm around Demon's shoulders. 'Give me the guided tour. Tell me about all these excellent creatures.'

By the time he'd taken the sea god up and down the stalls, warned him politely not to poke at the Giant Scorpion with the pointy end of his trident, and explained about the Cattle of the Sun not being able to eat ambrosia cake because of the terrible gas it gave them, Demon was feeling a bit more optimistic. Poseidon seemed much friendlier than the scary Hera, and a lot nicer than sinister Hades. Demon shivered, remembering his recent trip down to the Underworld to save the life of Hades' great beast-dog, Cerberus. He'd escaped being munched and crunched by the King of Death's skeleton dragons, thanks to the help of Hermes, the messenger god. But that wasn't the worst of it. If Hermes hadn't whisked him away right then and there, Demon would have gobbled down Queen Persephone's food and been trapped in the Underworld forever. Stopping at the last pen, he gestured at the ebony-coated winged horses within.

'These are the Ethiopian pegasi, Your Royal Godnificence,' he said, patting the shiny golden horns in the middle of the boss horse's forehead. 'I fly out on Keith here most days – pegasi need a lot of exercise to keep their wings strong.' Keith neighed enthusiastically as he nibbled on Demon's fingers.

'Horses, eh? What do you know of hippocamps, stable boy?' Poseidon asked abruptly.

Demon racked his brains. Hippocamps? What in the name of Zeus's toenails were they?

'I-I-I've never met one, Your Outstanding Oceanosity,' he said, feeling suddenly nervous again.

'No. I suppose you wouldn't have. I don't bring them up here much – no proper seawater, you see.' He clapped his hands together. 'Well, there's nothing for it. You'll just have to come back to the Stables of the Ocean with me and examine them. Their scales are all falling off, and none of my sea people seems to know why.'

Demon gulped and turned pale. He didn't know

what to do. How could he leave his own stables again? If there was no one to look after the beasts and clean them out, the whole of Olympus would smell of poo, and then the goddesses would get furious and turn him into one Demon-sized pile of ash. Poseidon frowned, his shaggy black eyebrows throwing off silvery-green sparks.

'You don't seem very happy, stable boy,' he growled. The atmosphere in the Stables of the Gods had suddenly become heavy and close, as if a big thunderstorm was rolling in. The winged horses whinnied in alarm as gusts of wind began to whip the dust up into mini tornadoes.

Demon hurriedly forced a smile onto his face. He'd just known Poseidon's nice mood was too good to last.

'N-no, n-no, Your Awesome Aquaticness, I-I-I was just w-wondering what medicines to bring. I-I'll go and fetch my box immediately.'

'Very well,' said Poseidon, his frown disappearing as suddenly as it had come and the wind subsiding. 'I'll go and visit my brother Zeus.

I have a small matter I need to discuss with him. Be ready when I return.'

With a swish and a swirl of his still-dripping cloak, the god left the stables, depositing a small shoal of flapping fish and a large angry lobster at Demon's feet. Demon leapt out of reach of the lobster's clacking claws and ran for the hospital shed. The griffin, after it had gobbled up the fish, loped after him on its lion's feet.

'Dearie me, Pan's scrawny kid,' Arnie sniggered, when it had caught up with him. 'Looks like you're in trouble whichever way you jump.'

'I know,' Demon panted as he ran. 'What am I going to DO, Arnie? What if he keeps me down there for ages? I can't just leave all of you on your own again. Look what happened with Doris last time. Aphrodite will probably turn me into a pile of burnt rose petals if her nighties start to smell of poo again.'

'We-e-e-ll,' said Arnie slowly, 'I suppose me and the Nemean Lion could make sure Doris does the clean-up and doesn't eat all the ambrosia cake again. The lion's been a bit depressed since you gave him that fluffy green skin. It'll cheer him up no end to have a job to do.'

'Would you really?' asked Demon, skidding to a halt in front of the hospital shed. 'I don't think it'll take very long. I'll be back in a day or so, I swear.' The griffin looked at him slyly out of the corner of its orange eye.

'Promise to give me meat at least once a week when you get back,' it said. 'Otherwise the deal's off.'

Demon groaned. Meat was really hard to come by on Olympus, unless it was a feast day. But he didn't really have a choice. He'd think about how to get round Arnie's request later. If Poseidon hadn't turned him into a Demon-shaped coral reef by then, of course.

'All right!' he said crossly. 'But, Arnie, you have to do the job properly. I don't want to find a piece of hay out of place, or a single speck of dust in any of the stalls. And I specially don't want to find Doris sick again. Understand?'

'Trust me, Pan's scrawny kid,' it said, giving him a sideways orange wink that made it look most *un*trustworthy. Then it flapped its eagle wings once, and soared up to sit on the rooftop. 'Better hurry up,' it called down. 'I see old Fishface coming out of Zeus's palace. He doesn't look in a very good mood.'

Demon's magical medicine box didn't turn out to be in a very good mood either when he told it they were going to Poseidon's watery realm. He could hear it grumbling behind him as it waddled its way towards the stables on its short, stumpy legs.

'Shut up, box,' he hissed as he saw Poseidon in the distance. 'You'll get us into trouble.'

'Implementing aqua-synchrous marine inter-face,' it muttered. 'As for you, I hope you get Error Code 7533 and turn into a sea cucumber.' The box withdrew its legs and thumped down beside him, ejecting a kind of see-through skin from its sides, that spread over its whole surface, even over the sticking-up handle, sealing it completely. Demon stared at it. How was he supposed to open the box now? But he had no time to think about that, because Poseidon was stomping towards him, muttering to himself. The air became thick and still again, and there was a strong smell of ozone.

'Come with me, stable boy,' the god said, gripping his arm with one ring-laden hand and pulling him towards Melanie's spring without another word. Demon grabbed the box's now slightly sticky-feeling handle and tugged. Slipping and sliding, it bounced behind Demon as he was dragged into the pool, sinking rapidly downwards before he could take more than one panicked, gulping breath of air.

# 2

# THE STABLES OF THE OCEAN

Demon held his breath for as long as he could, but eventually long streamers of silvery bubbles began to gush out of his mouth. He kicked and struggled frantically against the god's hold as he breathed in a big mouthful of seawater. Choking uncontrollably, his vision began to go black at the edges. *I'm going to drown*, he thought.

Just then Poseidon turned to look at him, his godly green eyes flashing as they took in what was happening. Whirling his trident round in one swift movement, he pointed it at Demon. Bright purple streaks shot from its three golden tips, weaving themselves swiftly into a net that dropped over Demon's head and body, encasing him completely before it sank into his skin and disappeared.

'Yeurrch! Yech! Yuck!' Demon wheezed. As Poseidon's magic began to change him, he started hacking up great gobs of slimy snot from the bottom of his quickly adapting lungs. Offy and Yukus, the two snakes that made up his magical healing necklace, curled and uncurled themselves anxiously round his neck. Demon just hoped they weren't going to get any ideas about plunging down his throat to suck more of the snot-slime out. He could manage to cough it up by himself, thank you very much!

'You weedy earthbound half-mortals,' said Poseidon, as they started to zoom down through the dark water again. 'No stamina, that's your trouble. You'll be all right now I've given you some of my sea power.'

Just as Demon was getting used to the strange sensation of breathing water as if it was air, his heart gave a panicky thump. In all the coughing and drowning bit, he'd somehow let go of his magic medical box. He craned desperately over one shoulder, trying to see it. A flash of silver caught his eye, just as he felt a bump at the back of his knees. The box had developed silvery fins and was swimming clumsily at his heels. He closed his eyes in relief. Thank goodness! Annoying as it was, there was no way he was going to cure a hippocamp without the box's help. Whatever a hippocamp was.

'Follow me, stable boy,' said Poseidon as they landed on the ocean floor. He swam off towards a rocky mountain covered in silver seaweed, Demon doggy-paddling awkwardly behind him. He wasn't used to swimming so fast, and rather wished he could grow fins like the box had. Quite soon he saw a wash of blue-green light in front of him. Two enormous golden doors stood open at the entrance to the mountain, guarded by two brawny creatures with green-skinned men's bodies, and scaly double fish tails on their bottom halves. They thumped their spears on the ground and snapped to rigid, tail-quivering attention as Poseidon swam past, Demon and the box behind him.

'All hail, Father of Oceans! All hail, King of the Seas,' they recited in a dreary monotone, making Demon jump.

'Yes, yes,' said Poseidon testily. 'No need for all that.' He bent his head down towards Demon. 'My Triton stable guards have loyal hearts, but few brains between them. Now, come on, stable boy. My poor hippocamps won't get any better if you just stand there gaping.'

They swam along a wide underwater corridor. Demon began to hear a muffled rustling, scraping sort of sound, and, as they turned a rocky corner, he saw a series of nine stalls made from many-coloured coral. Every stall was filled with a very odd-looking beast. Each had a shiny smooth-skinned white horse head and chest, and front legs that ended in dinner-plate-sized hooves surrounded by a ruff of spiny fins. Their backs and hindquarters were like monstrous fish, and their long golden spike-finned manes waved in the watery current. Demon could see the problem immediately. The round greenish-bronze scales that covered their rear ends were ragged and torn, and each hippocamp had big pink raw-looking patches where there were no scales at all.

'Oh! You poor things,' said Demon, swimming over to pat the nearest one, which promptly reared, squealed with rage and bared its large square teeth at him. 'Stop that,' he said in his firmest beast-taming voice. 'I'm here to help you.'

'Make them comfortable, stable boy,' ordered Poseidon. 'Find out what's wrong and fix it. You may ask one of the Tritons to bring you up to the throne room when you're finished. I have a meeting with Helios to go to now.' He paused, frowning, as a cloud of tiny golden fish zipped in and out of his beard. 'Can't think what my wretched sky cousin wants with me. Fire and water don't mix, you know.' With that, he launched himself upwards and shot through an opening in the coral roof.

Demon sighed. Although the sea god hadn't threatened to turn him into a pile of powdered seaweed, he didn't need telling that things wouldn't go well for him if he didn't find a cure for the hippocamps.

'Right, box,' he said, turning round. 'We have work to do. Let's find out what's wrong with these poor beasts.' But the box had disappeared. 'Box!' he said again, peering into the dark corners of the Stables of the Ocean. 'Box! Stop sulking and come here at once.' There was no reply. Trying not to panic, Demon looked in every stall, and checked behind every rock. Then he swam back down the passage to the golden doors. 'Have you seen my silver box?' he asked the Tritons. They shook their heads.

Demon wanted to kick something. It was so unfair! He wished he'd never been taken away from his mum and made to do this stupid job. He was swimming back towards the stable again, thinking gloomy thoughts about all the horrible things Poseidon was going to do to him, when he heard a shout behind him.

'Lost something?' asked a high little voice.

Paddling round clumsily, Demon saw a girl in a floaty blue robe. She had very pale green skin, legs that ended in two neat flipper feet, and two braids of long dark green hair wound round her head, firmly clipped in place by several pairs of golden crabs. Her cheeky grin showed a mouthful of small pearly teeth and in her arms she was holding a struggling silver box.

'Oh, thank goodness!' Demon said. 'Where did you find it?'

The girl blushed a deeper shade of green. 'Well,' she replied, looking slightly guilty. 'I saw a big silver box lying about doing nothing. And I thought the Queen might like it for keeping her spare crowns in. So I kind of stole it. Only . . . only then it sort of came alive and told me I'd be in trouble with Poseidon if I didn't bring it back here to the stables. So I thought I'd better do what it said. I don't want to be turned into a whale monster! He did that to one of my cousins, and now he's a giant ugly brute.'

'Just as well,' said Demon, twin surges of anger and relief shooting through him. 'If I'd lost it, you wouldn't have been the only one Poseidon turned into something horrible. Now give it here. I've wasted enough time.' He swam forward and grabbed the box, giving it a little pat of thanks before heading back towards the hippocamps. The girl followed him.

'What are you doing?' she asked.

'Trying to cure Poseidon's poorly hippocamps, of course,' he said, rather carefully approaching the one who'd tried to bite him. 'Can't you see their scales are all falling off? Now go away. I'm a bit busy, in case you hadn't noticed.'

The girl didn't move.

'I know the magic hippocamp trick,' she said, watching thoughtfully as the creature bared its teeth again and laid back its smooth green-bronze ears. 'If you're interested.'

The hippocamp snaked out its head faster than Zeus's lightning and clamped its jaws round Demon's arm, its blue eyes rolling.

'Aarrghh!' he yelled, jumping backwards and leaving a large chunk of his flesh behind. Immediately Offy and Yukus slithered off his neck and twined themselves round the wound, which stung doubly from the salt water. The magic snakes sealed and healed it, and as soon as it had stopped hurting he turned to look at her. 'What magic hippocamp trick?' he asked, his voice full of suspicion. He wasn't going to trust someone who'd admitted to stealing his magic box *that* easily.

'This,' she replied, gliding over to the sea horse, seizing it by the nostrils and twisting gently before it had a chance to react. Moving fast, she brought its head close to her face and quickly blew a stream of bubbles up its nose. At once its eyelids drooped, and it went all dopey. Demon was impressed in spite of himself. It was as good as playing his father's magical pan pipes. The girl turned towards him, a slightly smug look on her face.

'You can examine him properly now. He'll stay calm for a while. I'm Eunice, by the way, daughter of Nereus, and one of the nereids.'

'I'm Demon,' he said, holding out a hand. 'Official Beastkeeper to the Gods on Olympus, and son of Pan. Nice to meet you.'

Eunice giggled, holding out her own webbed hand and shaking his. 'We don't do that down here, we wiggle ours instead. But it's nice to meet you too, Demon. And even nicer that you're not one of my forty-nine stupid sisters. I'm so bored of their fancy jewellery-trying-on parties and silly gossip. I want to do something interesting. I wish I could have a proper job like you – I'd love to look after the hippocamps. I'd be better at it than those stupid Tritons, anyway!'

'Well, I guess you can help me with this lot, then,' Demon said. 'But we'd better hurry. I don't want to find out what Poseidon will do if I don't report back to him soon.' With that, he turned to the medical box, which was hovering by his left elbow. 'I need a cure for these hippocamps, please. Right now, if possible.'

The box began to flash blue as it flapped its fins and moved closer to the still dopey beast. The see-through skin covering it bulged slightly, and a tube with a suction cup emerged from under the just-open lid, moving over the ragged, peeling scales with a slurping sound before sliding back inside.

'What *is* that thing?' asked Eunice, her pale aquamarine eyes widening as she watched.

'Hephaestus made it for me. You know, the blacksmith god? The one who makes all the magic armour for the Olympians? He's really good at inventing stuff.' Demon was about to explain what the box did, when it started to make whirring noises and flash again. 'Here it goes. We'll have a cure in a minute,' he said, crossing his fingers hopefully.

'Running preliminary diagnostics,' said the box, its tinny tones sounding muffled under its waterproof covering.

'What's "preliminary diagnostics"?' Eunice asked.

'Take no notice,' said Demon. 'It uses fancy terms to make it sound clever – but mostly because it likes to annoy me. Diagnostics just means it's looking for the right medicine.'

The box spat a blue spark and made what sounded suspiciously like a snort.

'Hipponautikos akropyodermatitis detected in subject,' it said. Demon glared at it. 'More commonly known as Persistent Itchy-itch,' it added hurriedly.

'Itchy,' the hippocamp whinnied drowsily. Its eyes snapped open. 'ITCHY!' it screamed.

**'ITCHYitchyITCHYitchyITCHY!'**

Then it flung itself backwards, writhing and wriggling its scales against the walls. Immediately its stablemates joined in, until the whole cave was filled with an echoing chorus of horrible hippocamp screams and the harsh sound of scales being rubbed off against coral.

# 3

# A GODLY FIGHT

'STOP IT!' yelled Demon.

But it was no good, the hippocamps were in a dreadful frenzy of agonising itchiness. Neither he nor Eunice could get anywhere near them to blow soothing bubbles up their noses – there were too many flailing fishtails and razor-sharp hooves flying about to even try. Demon fumbled in the front of his chiton and pulled out his dad Pan's magic pipes, hoping against hope that they'd work underwater. Cramming them against his lips, he blew hard. A swirl of silver music curled out, quite visible against the churning turbulence around the terrified sea beasts. It split into nine parts and shot forward, coiling around each hippocamp's muzzle like a halter. There was an immediate silence. Every one of the nine panicked creatures sighed deeply, closed its blue eyes and fell fast asleep.

'Wow!' said Eunice. 'That's way cooler than my trick!'

Demon didn't waste a moment.

'Quick, box,' he said. 'I need a cure right now, before they all wake up again.'

For once the box didn't argue. The shiny membrane that covered it strained and swelled, and a large copper-coloured pot of ointment erupted from its lid with a loud *POP*.

'Apply liberally to all areas,' said the box. Then, with a wheezing sound, it closed and shut down, sinking to the sandy floor of the cave. Demon grabbed the pot and wrenched at the lid. It wouldn't budge.

'Come on,' he said. 'Come ON! Open, you Zeus-blasted thing!'

'Here,' said Eunice, swimming forward to help him. 'I'll hold, you twist.'

Demon strained and grunted, and at last, with an ear-splitting *CLUNK,* the top came off. As soon as the pot was open, they dug their hands into the gloopy yellow gunk inside and started to smear it over the sleeping hippocamps' scales.

'I really hope this works,' said Demon. 'Because I never want to hear those hippocamps screaming again. It was AWFUL.'

'I know,' Eunice agreed. 'Even a pack of hunting telchines doesn't sound as bad as that.'

Demon sighed. Was this yet another kind of beast he hadn't heard of?

'What are telchines?' he asked as he smeared and daubed at hippocamp scales. Eunice looked around nervously.

'I shouldn't really have mentioned them,' she whispered. 'They're Poseidon's secret punishment squad. They've got monster-dog heads and seal flippers, and they never lose the trail of someone they're after.' She shuddered. 'I've only ever seen them on the hunt once. Believe me, you're better off not meeting them. They're terrifying.'

'I'm pretty good with beasts,' Demon said, boasting a bit. 'I even tamed Hades' earth dragons, so I don't suppose a few telchines would scare me. They don't sound all that bad. No worse than the Giant Scorpion, anyway.'

Eunice just looked at him. Clearly the boasting hadn't impressed her much.

'Don't say I didn't warn you,' she said, wiping the last of the ointment off her hands. Just then, the first of the hippocamps gave a sleepy nicker. Demon crossed his fingers and toes. Would the ointment have worked yet? Maybe the hippocamps would be hungry when they woke up. He looked around him, noticing several bales of silver seaweed piled up in one corner.

'Is that what they eat?' he asked, pointing. Eunice nodded. 'Well, at least it's not leftover ambrosia cake,' he said. 'That would go disgustingly soggy down here.'

As they swam around, filling each manger, Eunice shot a barrage of questions at him about the Stables of the Gods and Mount Olympus. How many beasts did he have to look after? (A lot.) Why didn't he like ambrosia cake? (Because it was boring eating it day after day – and it tasted horrible!) What was the most difficult thing he'd ever had to cure? (Doris the Hydra and its cut-off heads.) Demon hadn't talked so much in ages, and he found he liked being with someone his own age a lot.

'Eunice . . .' he started, wanting to ask her more about telchines. But just then the hippocamps woke up all at once, plunged their noses into the full mangers and started munching.

'Look!' she squealed, clapping her webbed hands. 'They're getting better!'

Demon looked. Their scales were gleaming and healthy once more, with tiny new golden-bronze ones starting to fill in the now-healed pink patches.

'Oh! Thank Zeus's left armpit,' he said. There

was a small cough from the floor. Demon glanced down. 'Oh, all right. Thank you too, box.' The box glowed a pleased kind of blue and flapped its fins. 'Now, come on, we'd better go and find one of those Tritons to take us to Poseidon.'

Eunice rolled her eyes. 'Stupid Tritons. I bet the hippocamps got sick because those idiots weren't looking after them properly. It wouldn't have happened if I'd been in charge, I can tell you. Don't worry – I'll take you to the throne room. I'd better join my stupid sisters again anyway, or I'll be in trouble, and that's where they'll be.'

Chattering on, Eunice led the way upwards through the hole in the cave ceiling. Demon followed, trying to copy the graceful, easy way she swam without much success. As he floundered at her heels, he rather wished Poseidon had given him flippers as well as underwater breathing.

He was concentrating so hard on his swimming that he didn't get any warning when Eunice stopped dead in front of him.

'*OOF!*' she gasped as he rammed right into her

back, knocking her head over heels and up through an arched doorway. With no warning, both their heads broke through the surface of a gleaming pool and hit air. Both the air and the brighter light of the glittering cavern he was now in were a shock to Demon after being underwater for so long. He was blinking, and gasping loudly as his lungs adapted back from breathing seawater. Eunice seized him by the hand and dragged him behind a pillar.

'Shh!' she hissed fiercely. 'Look!' Demon took a breath of damp air and gazed about him with wide, awed eyes. Above the gleaming pool, he saw an endlessly high deep-blue arched ceiling, decorated with sparkling diamonds to imitate the night sky above the ocean. The smooth walls glowed the exact shade of the inside of a pearly oyster shell . . . and there was a small crowd of sea people pressed back against them, all looking terrified. In the very centre of the cavern, raised above the water, was a high dais, with a throne placed on it which seemed to be carved out of one giant sapphire, and in front of the throne stood two gods, nose to nose and clearly extremely angry. Demon suddenly noticed that the water had got very hot around him.

'Say that again!' roared Poseidon, his black beard bristling as the water roiled and bubbled, slopping small waves onto the rocky platform below the throne.

'My celestial horses can beat your stupid slow hippocamps any day of the week,' yelled a purple-robed god with a golden crown of sunrays on his head. It was Helios, god of the sun. Beams of heat shot out from his eyes, turning the light in the cavern orangey-yellow and the water even hotter.

'Gentlegods, gentlegods, there's only one way to settle this,' said a voice, apparently coming from nowhere, a voice Demon knew very well. The messenger god Hermes took off his invisibility hat and strolled out of thin air towards the two furious gods of sea and sun. 'You two must challenge each other to a race. I suggest a course once around the earth – one taking the sea route, and the other going by sky. Invite all the gods and goddesses to watch and witness – and the victor gives a feast.'

As Hermes spoke, the water in the pool below the three gods calmed and became cooler.

'Very well,' said Poseidon, stalking back to his throne and sitting down. 'Consider the challenge given, Sun Dragger.'

'Done,' said Helios. 'I'll meet you seven days from now, Father of Fishiness. Prepare to lose that golden trident of yours!' With that, he let out a blast of blinding light and disappeared.

'Wretched jumped-up Titan,' muttered Poseidon, his black eyebrows twitching into a fierce frown. 'Always trying to pick a fight since the day I won the city of Corinth from him.' The water in the throne room pool darkened and began to churn again. Several sea nymphs and mermaids squeaked and fled.

'Come on, dear Uncle,' said Hermes soothingly. 'I've seen those hippocamps of yours. They're fast, and if you rest them well, they should beat Helios easily. Don't forget, those celestial horses of his will be pulling the sun behind them – they won't exactly be fresh.'

'Hmmm,' said Poseidon. 'Well, my hippocamps aren't exactly on top form either. At least they weren't. Maybe Zeus's stable boy has managed to cure them. Where is the wretched brat anyway? He should have reported in by now.'

Eunice gave Demon a little shove forward.

'Go on,' she whispered. 'Tell him the good news. It might make him in a better temper.'

Demon swam clumsily forward through the pool.

'Er, I'm here, Your Opulent Oceanosity,' he said, clinging onto the rocks below the throne as Hermes winked at him encouragingly. 'Your hippocamps are doing well. Their scales are growing back nicely and they're eating like . . . well . . . like horses.'

Poseidon scowled at him. 'They'd better be fine,' he growled. 'Or I'll have you on your knees scrubbing salt off seaweed for the next hundred years. Consider yourself assigned to the Stables of the Ocean till further notice. I want my hippocamps in tip-top condition for the race. You're looking after them full-time till then.'

Demon's heart gave a horrible blip and sank right down to his toes. What sort of state would his own stables be in after a whole week? He'd sworn to Arnie that he'd be back in a couple of days – he didn't trust the griffin and the Nemean Lion to cope for any longer than that, anyway. What WAS he going to do? Giving Hermes a look of complete desperation, he bowed to Poseidon and stammered out the only thing he thought might stop the god turning him into a coral reef.

'Y-yes, Y-your M-mighty G-godnificence. I'll get down there and see to it at once.'

# 4
# HERMES TO THE RESCUE

*Please, Hermes, please,* Demon prayed to the messenger god over and over again, *I really, really need to talk to you.* But Hermes stayed firmly in the middle of the throne room, chatting away to Poseidon in his usual light-hearted manner. As Demon swam slowly back towards where he'd left Eunice the water became calm and cool again, and he could hear chattering voices ahead of him and squeals of girlish laughter.

'Ooh! Here he is!'

'Isn't he cute?'

'Why don't you introduce us to your *boyfriend*, Eunice?'

Suddenly he was surrounded by a whole gaggle of nereid girls, each dressed in a different-coloured floaty robe. It was like being in the middle of a garden of sea flowers, and Demon felt himself blushing as Eunice took him firmly by the arm.

'Girls, this is Demon. Demon, these are my sisters, Maira, Neso, Erato, Halia . . .' She stopped. 'Oh, never mind. You'll never remember all forty-nine of them, and they're too silly to bother with anyway.' She pulled him out of the circle of admiring glances and giggles and turned to face them. 'Now go away and polish pearls or something. I've got to show Demon the way back to the stables.'

Pouting, the pack of girls swam away. One of them turned back, shaking her finger at Eunice.

'Just wait till I tell Amphitrite about you, Eunice. She'll be cross if you're not there to brush her hair at bedtime. You're meant to be a nymph-in-waiting to the Queen, not helping some stupid stable boy.'

'I don't care, Thetis,' said Eunice defiantly. 'You know I like being with sea beasts more than brushing royal hair. And he's not stupid. Come on, Demon, let's go.'

By this time, Demon's face was redder than a ripe cherry. Why did girls always have to be so giggly and weird? Why couldn't they just act normal? He wrenched his arm out of Eunice's grip.

'I'll be fine,' he said, now horribly embarrassed. 'You don't need to come. I can manage to find my own way.'

Eunice's face fell.

'Oh. W-well, all right, then. I just thought . . .' She looked so downcast that Demon immediately felt guilty.

'I didn't mean . . .'

'I only . . .'

'You go first,' said Eunice, still looking upset. Demon could see he needed to help her feel better.

'I didn't mean to hurt your feelings,' he said.

'It's just . . . your sisters . . . Queen Amphitrite . . . I don't want to get you in trouble . . .' He gestured helplessly, suddenly not sure what to say.

'Really? Is that all? Oh, never mind them. I told you they were silly, remember? And Queen Amphitrite will let me off if I explain.' Her face turned a deeper green, and Demon realised she was blushing too. 'I-I-I thought it might be because you didn't like me. My sisters always say I'm much too bossy for my own good, but I was only trying to help. I'd really like to be friends with you if you'll let me.' Demon breathed a sigh of relief. Friends was just fine by him, and he could definitely use all the help he could get.

'Friends,' he agreed, holding out his hand and waggling it at her. 'Is this how you do it?'

Eunice laughed.

Pretty much,' she said, flapping her webbed one in return.

The hippocamps had eaten all their silver seaweed by the time they got down to the Stables of the

Ocean, so Eunice and Demon set about refilling the mangers. Just as they were finishing, Demon heard a loud whistle and Hermes dropped through the hole in the ceiling.

'Fancy seeing you here, stable boy,' said the messenger god, his usual mischievous grin spread all over his face. 'Did a little seashell whisper that you might be needing me? Are you in trouble AGAIN?'

'Yes,' said Demon, too relieved to see him to bother with politeness. 'Or I will be if I leave the Stables of the Gods with Arnie and the Nemean Lion in charge for too much longer – and Poseidon wants me to stay here for a whole week. You know what happened last time.'

'I do indeed. We can't have the whole of Olympus smelling of poo again or the goddesses will be after you.' Hermes tapped one long fingernail against his very white teeth, clearly thinking. 'Tell you what. I have a young man called Autolycus who's in a bit of bother at the moment over some cattle he stole. He's not bad with beasts and he owes me a favour or two. I expect he'd look after the stables for a week. He's a cunning little chap.'

Demon tried to picture a clever thief looking after the Giant Scorpion and failed miserably. But what other choice did he have?

'Thank you, Hermes,' he said gratefully. Then he had an awful thought. What if this Autolycus person got badly bitten, or even stung, by the Giant Scorpion? He'd need protection. Putting a hand to his neck he unfastened his magical snake necklace. 'Maybe I'd better lend him Offy and Yukus. Otherwise he might get killed. Some of my beasts aren't very friendly, you know. And what about Hephaestus's box? Shouldn't he have that too?'

'No, no,' said Hermes. 'You keep all that. I'll make sure he's safe, don't worry. You just get on with looking after these fine beasties. Now, I've got places to be, people to see. Bye for now!' With a wave of his hand, the god put on his invisibility hat and vanished.

'Goodness!' Eunice whispered. 'Was that really

Hermes? Only . . . only he doesn't seem like a g . . . I mean . . .' Her voice stuttered to a halt, but Demon knew exactly what she'd been going to say.

'Doesn't seem like a god?' he asked. She nodded. 'Well, no, he doesn't. At least not some of the other ones I've met. I'm always scared they're going to turn me into little piles of ash – apart from Heffy and Hestia – but Hermes is really n—'

Before he could finish his sentence, however, Eunice had darted into a cleft in the rock, cowering with fear, and a second later he saw why. Poseidon swam into the cave with a rush of dark water. Demon fell to his knees beside the silver box.

'H-h-hello, Your Serene Saltiness,' he said.

Poseidon gestured impatiently.

'Get up, get up. All this wretched bowing and scraping drives me mad. Now, let me see how my lovely hippocamps are doing.' Crooning in a most unkinglike way, he went from stall to stall, patting noses and stroking spiky manes. 'Well, well. They seem quite recovered.'

The sea god clapped Demon on the shoulder, sending him shooting backwards through the water. 'Good job, stable boy, you deserve a reward. Now, let's harness them up and put them through their paces. I'll show you why I'm going to win this race.'

As Poseidon showed Demon where his racing chariot was and how to harness the nine hippocamps to it, Eunice remained huddled in her rocky hideaway, putting a green finger to her lips, She was obviously too scared to come out, so Demon tried not to look at her, not wanting to give her away as he and the sea god did up buckles and threaded straps together. That was a big surprise – Hades had made Demon do all the hard work of harnessing the earth dragons – but the King of the Ocean seemed to like doing it himself. Finally, the chariot was ready.

'In you get,' said Poseidon, pointing to the seat behind him. Demon climbed in rather nervously. The last chariot he'd been in was Hera's, and that hadn't been a good experience at all. They'd rushed down to earth to rescue Doris the Hydra from a dreadful death at the hands of horrible Heracles, and the Queen of the Gods had been in a blistering rage with everyone and everything – including Demon.

This chariot was rather different. It was made in the shape of a long streamlined silver shell, and had two low bucket seats lined with cushions of soft, spongy red sea moss. Poseidon was strapping himself into one with two thick strands of green ribbon kelp, which passed round his shoulders and were clipped with two large silver crabs to a third, which went between his legs. 'Buckle up, stable boy,' he barked. 'And prepare for the ride of your life.'

Scrambling into the seat behind him, Demon had just managed to figure out how the kelp harness fitted together when Poseidon cracked his trident like a whip. A jet of purple light snaked out over the hippocamps' heads, and with a joyful whinny they were off. Demon caught a glimpse of Eunice's scared eyes flashing past before he was jolted back in his seat and clinging on to his kelp straps with both hands. The hippocamps rushed through the golden doors and past the Triton guards, and then Poseidon cracked his trident again.

'Yee-haw, giddy up,' he yelled happily, his black hair streaming out behind him like seaweed. The hippocamps went even faster, till all Demon could see of the underwater world rushing past him was a series of blurred streaks. Up and up and up they went until they broke the surface of the sea. With a gasp, Demon was breathing air again, and then they were skimming across the top of a calm deep blue ocean, the hippocamps' long spiky manes flying like golden foam in the breeze.

# 5

# THE HORSES OF THE SUN

Demon never did manage to catch his breath properly on that wild, amazing ride. Poseidon urged his steeds to go faster and faster, and by the time they sank beneath the waves again, Demon's hands were so cramped and uncomfortable from hanging on to his straps that he thought they might never unclench. The change from air to water was still a little strange, but he was getting used to it now.

The sea god looked at him sideways as he slowed

the hippocamps down and guided them gently back to the Stables of the Ocean.

'So, stable boy. How was that for you?'

Demon grinned at the god before he could stop himself. It HAD been very exciting as well as totally terrifying!

'Er, stupendous, Your Serene Saltiness. I think you're going to win. They're really quick, aren't they?'

'Quicker than anything in sea, sky or earth, and don't you forget it. Now, unharness them and give them a good rub down with a sea sponge. Then polish up their scales with some sea-slug slime. They'll need as much seaweed as they can eat, and then later we'll take them over to my other palace at Macris. That's where the race is going to start from. Got it?' Demon nodded as Poseidon shot up through the hole in the ceiling.

'Yes, Your Mighty Marineness,' he said to the god's disappearing toes. Once he was sure he was alone, he peered around him. 'Eunice!' he hissed. 'Eunice, where are you? You can come out now.'

But there was no reply. Eunice was gone, and he had no idea where to find her – or any of the things Poseidon had mentioned. There wasn't a sea sponge to be seen anywhere, let alone any sea-slug slime. He led each hippocamp back to its pen, hung the harness up, and pushed the racing chariot back to the small cave it had come from, wondering what he was going to do. Then he looked at the hippocamp who'd bitten him and had an idea.

'Could you tell me where the stable supplies are, please?' he asked politely. But the hippocamp just rolled its blue eye at him menacingly and let out a loud whinny.

'Sponge,' it neighed. 'Slime. Seaweed.' Then the whole lot of them started.

'SPONGE. SLIME. SEAWEED,' they chorused.

They might be fast, Demon thought, but they hadn't so much as a brain cell between them.

'All right, all right! I'll find them myself,' he shouted above the noise. But search as he might, he couldn't find anything but the seaweed. Tipping it into the mangers shut the hippocamps up, but he knew he probably hadn't got much time before they started making a racket again. With a tired sigh, he sat down on a coral outcrop next to the magic medical box.

'Don't suppose you've seen any of that stuff Poseidon mentioned, have you, box?'

The box didn't answer, but a beam of blue shot out from its lid, lighting up the murky water in the darkest corner of the stables. Demon got up to investigate, even though he was sure he'd looked there before. By the box's light, he saw what looked like a cupboard door in the rocky wall, with a tiny doorknob in the shape of a starfish. Wrenching it open, he was very happy indeed to discover everything he needed inside.

Armed with sponges, he rubbed down each hippocamp in turn, using Eunice's clever trick of blowing up the nostrils of any that looked like nipping him. Then he turned to the big pot of sea-slug slime. It was thick and green and gloopy, and if he wasn't careful putting it on the sponge, great globs of it floated off and stuck to his chiton.

He was just glad that his sense of smell didn't work underwater, because it looked absolutely revolting. The hippocamps' scales were fully grown back now, and by the time he'd finished with them they looked shiny and beautiful, and he was utterly exhausted. It had been a very long day, and he'd had nothing to eat. Curling up on some seaweed in a corner, and trying not to think about his starving stomach, Demon fell fast asleep.

He was woken by a gentle nudge on the shoulder.

'Go 'way, Arnie,' he groaned, still half asleep, and forgetting where he was. There was a further, slightly less gentle nudge to his ribs. Demon's eyes snapped open. There in front of him, instead of the griffin, was a creature with kind eyes and a mouth half open in a friendly grin. It had two flippers, and six starry points of light along its long, smooth body, making the whole cavern shine with a warm glow, and it was the most beautiful thing Demon had ever seen.

'Up you get, son of Pan,' it said. 'Queen

Amphitrite wants to see you. Hop on and I'll take you to her.' It gestured with a flipper to its back.

Demon rubbed his sleepy eyes and yawned, wondering what the queen wanted with him, and what this creature was.

'All right,' he said. 'But I'd better feed this lot first. I don't want Poseidon getting angry with me.'

'Wise decision,' said the creature. 'But hurry up. You don't want to keep the queen waiting either!'

Demon hurried to fill the mangers yet again, then clambered up onto the long, smooth back, hanging on to the big curved fin.

'Er, who are you, if you don't mind me asking?' he said, as they swam upwards, the creature's powerful body twisting and turning under him, making the lights within it flash and flicker like jewels.

'I'm Delphinus,' it said. 'Messenger Dolphin to the Queen. Now hang on and keep your head down. I'm taking us up by the short cut.'

Demon crouched low as the dolphin raced this way and that through narrow tunnels and passageways, eventually shooting out into another brightly lit cavern and surfacing. Shafts of sunlight poured in through long, high windows, open to the sea breeze, and reflected off a pool of still water, turning it golden. The air in this cavern felt cold and clean and fresh in his lungs.

In the middle of the pool was a large island, covered in soft green moss. Demon's heart sank into his bare toes as he saw a crowd of brightly coloured robes and recognised Eunice's giggling sisters. Reclining on a low couch among them lay Queen Amphitrite, with Eunice behind her, brushing out one side of the queen's long dark blue hair while her sister Nereid braided tiny jewelled sea anemones into the other.

'Ouch!' cried the queen crossly. 'Why do you always have to pull my hair so, Eunice?'

'Here he is, Your Majesty,' said Delphinus, giving a wriggle so that Demon tipped off the dolphin's back and splashed into the golden pool.

Amphitrite pointed to a low stool beside her with one webbed finger.

'Swim over and sit there,' she said, her voice now low and husky, like tiny pebbles washing against the shore. As Demon clambered out of the water and tried to wring his chiton dry, his tummy rumbled loudly. 'Are you hungry, son of Pan?'

Demon nodded eagerly. He was hungrier than a starving starfish. 'Yes, Your Majesty,' he said, trying not to drool too obviously.

Amphitrite smiled at him as Delphinus swam off again.

'Halia, fetch our guest something to eat and drink.' One of the nereids went over to a small table, and brought Demon a cup of green juice and a platter piled high with delicious-looking morsels.

'Here you are, Demon,' she said, fluttering her long green eyelashes at him in a rather worrying way. Demon was too hungry to care about silly girls, though. He concentrated on not stuffing everything into his mouth at once instead. He wasn't too sure how goddesses felt about table manners, but if Amphitrite was anything like his mum, it was probably best not to gobble like a wild beast.

'I want to know all the gossip from Olympus,' said Amphitrite, when Demon had cleaned his plate for the third time. 'Who's annoyed Hera lately? Is it true about Eos's poor husband being turned into a grasshopper? Did Apollo really give that stupid Midas asses' ears?'

Demon's ears turned redder than cooked lobsters.

'I . . . I don't really hear much gossip in the stables, Your Briny Bountifulness,' he said. 'Well, only what Althea, Melanie and Melia say about . . . w-w-well . . .' He stuttered into silence, but Amphitrite just waved a pale blue webbed hand at him, jewelled fingernails flashing in the reflected sunlight.

'Tell me all!' she purred.

'Yes, do,' sighed Eunice's sisters, sinking down at the sea queen's feet like a shoal of colourful fish, and gazing up at him expectantly. Blushing, he looked desperately at Eunice for help, but she just grinned at him, shrugged and kept on brushing her royal mistress's hair.

A long and very uncomfortable time later, Amphitrite had winkled out every morsel of information Demon had about the doings of the gods and goddesses on Olympus. She yawned, stretching like a sinuous eel, just as a loud hooting sound sounded somewhere outside, making Demon jump nervously. He was about to ask what it was when he heard a pair of familiar-sounding voices shouting.

'Make way for the Father of the Oceans, make way for the King of the Seas,' bellowed the Tritons, their monotonous tones ringing round the chamber as they flung open the double doors. Amphitrite rose from her couch, glossy blue hair tumbling down her back like a shiny waterfall. She curtsied, and held out a hand to Poseidon.

'Welcome, my King,' she said, smiling at her husband.

'Nearly ready to go, my dear?' he asked, striding across the top of the water towards her, his golden trident strapped across his back. Then his eyes fell on Demon, kneeling at the queen's feet. He frowned, and the room grew darker. Small wavelets began to run around the pool, slapping against the moss. 'What's that stable boy doing in your chambers?' he boomed, staring at Demon suspiciously. 'He's meant to be looking after my hippocamps, not lounging about up here!'

'Don't be cross, my cockleshell,' said Amphitrite, putting a hand on his arm. 'I asked him up here. You know how I am about having the very latest news from Olympus – and he had some very juicy titbits of gossip to offer!'

Demon nearly groaned out loud. They hadn't been that juicy – he'd only mentioned what Althea had told him about Hera turning poor Io the nymph into a cow, but the queen had seemed to find that *very* interesting. He had no idea why.

'Very well,' said Poseidon. 'But I want him back now. There's a lot of packing up for him to do before we leave for Macris.' He frowned again, but less ferociously. 'Off you go now, boy. I'll send one of the Tritons with you to help.'

Demon felt a sharp elbow prod his side, and turned to see Eunice glaring at him pointedly. He knew exactly what she wanted him to say before she even mouthed 'I want to come' at him.

'Er, Your M-Majesties,' he said bravely, taking a deep breath and blurting it all out in a rush. 'W-would it be all right if I had my friend Eunice as my helper for the rest of the day? She's . . . she's very good with the hippocamps.'

Poseidon let out a sudden lightning crack of laughter.

'Good with the hippocamps is she, stable boy?' He peered down at Eunice, who was half hiding behind Demon. 'Ah! Young Eunice! Aren't you the one my Tritons complain is always hanging about the stables?' Eunice nodded, looking scared. 'Well, never mind that. Pandemonius, you can have her if my queen agrees . . .' He raised one bushy black eyebrow at Amphitrite.

'Oh, very well,' she said. 'She's already tugged my hair around enough for one day. But if there's even a trace of hippocamp slime anywhere near my best hairbrush when she comes back tonight, I shall turn you both into a pair of purple clownfish. Now, be off with you.' She turned and flounced back to her couch, clearly displeased.

'Yes, Your Majesty,' said Eunice. 'I mean, no, Your Majesty. Er . . . I mean, I promise there won't be . . .' Then she curtsied hurriedly, turned, and fled. Demon was close behind her, managing to stuff a few more delicious goodies into his mouth as he went. He wasn't at all sure when he'd next get anything to eat.

# 6

# THE PALACE AT MACRIS

There was a frantic bustle of activity in the corridors as Eunice and Demon dodged past gigantic octopus servants with tentacles full of boxes and baskets, and a flurry of sea people swimming this way and that, shouting orders and generally getting in each other's way.

By the time they reached the underwater stables, Demon was too puffed to speak, gasping and gurgling as his lungs adjusted again. The hippocamps were in a high state of excitement, neighing loudly and rearing as Demon and Eunice ran about packing the harness, grooming equipment and bales of silvery seaweed, lashing it all down with kelp ropes on to several long, low sleds which had been left out for them. It took hours and hours. Just as Demon was tying down his medical box (which was shouting loudly that it could perfectly well swim by itself) onto the last sled, several mermen swam in, leading strange long-nosed fish-beasts, which grinned at them with mouths full of sharp white teeth. Their red backs were covered in arrow-like spines, and huge undulating tails swished the water around their pale, gleaming bellies.

'Ready?' asked one of the mermen in a deep, gruff voice. Demon nodded, backing away warily as the mermen wrangled kelp harnesses round the creatures' huge front fins, attaching them to the sleds.

'What are *those*?' he whispered to Eunice.

'Oh, just some of the smaller whale-monsters,' she said. 'They're very friendly really – as long as you don't feed them oysters. That sends them a bit crazy. My sister Keto is supposed to be in charge of them – but she's so lazy she lets the mermen do most of the work.' She looked over at him, as the last sleds floated out of the stables, muffled protests from the silver box still drifting back towards them. 'Thanks for letting me come with you. I just wish Poseidon would let me —' She broke off suddenly as Poseidon himself appeared in a swirl of sea foam, and by the time Demon had finished harnessing the hippocamps to the sea god's chariot, Eunice had disappeared again. But he had no time to think about that as the god hurried him into the chariot and the hippocamps drew them up to the surface of the sea and swiftly over the waves to the sea god's earthly home on the island of Macris.

Poseidon's other palace was a pleasant surprise. It was built on both land and sea, with endless rocky turrets and coral battlements, and silvery-blue walls soaring up from the waves. Once Poseidon had given him his instructions on how he wanted the hippocamps fed and exercised for the next few days, Demon started to settle them down in their new home. The stables were in a light, airy cave, with spacious underwater stalls where the hippocamps could splash about to their hearts' content, and places to store everything they needed. There was even a tiny dry alcove in the cave roof with a small sleeping pallet and a blanket woven of soft seagrass. Later on, when he'd piled each manger high with silver seaweed, Demon finally set out to explore the island. It felt good to wiggle his bare toes in the soft, springy grass, and feel the herb-scented breeze on his face. Being underwater was all very well for a bit, but he'd definitely missed the fresh air and the smell of the earth.

Unfortunately, just as he was walking back along the cliff tops to see if the sleds of supplies had arrived, he had a nasty surprise. The sun was setting in a blaze of red and pink cloud, when a bright light began to shine on the path in front of him. Demon stopped and stared as the bright light took on the shape of a door, and a tall, golden-haired god with a crown of sunrays stepped through it. It was Helios, Poseidon's deadly race rival. Demon stared, his mouth hanging open. How in Zeus's name had he done that? Surely even gods couldn't just make doors in the air wherever they wanted?

'Why, if it isn't young Pandemonius,' Helios said, baring his square, white teeth in a friendly grin that somehow looked menacing. 'Like my little trick, do you?'

Demon nodded. Well, it *was* pretty amazing.

The god lowered his head. 'Not many people know my secret,' he whispered. 'But I'm sure you'll keep it to yourself. You see, I can make a door anywhere the sun's rays can touch. Useful, eh?' Demon nodded again, as Helios took his elbow in a firm grip so he couldn't escape. 'Now, you're just the boy I wanted. We have important things to discuss.'

Demon's stomach tried to leap sideways in fright. In his experience, discussing important things with a god almost always led to trouble.

The kind of trouble that left him worrying about being frazzled to a frizzle.

'The thing is,' said the sun god. 'I have a small problem. Here you are, looking after old Father Fishface's hippocamps, but, as I understand it, you're Official Beastkeeper to the Gods, aren't you? *Gods*, meaning more than one god . . .'

'W-w-well y-yes, Y-y-your Sh-sh-shining S-s-serenity,' Demon gulped. 'I-I s-suppose I am.' Helios smiled again. It was not a nice smile at all. Demon's knees began to tremble.

'Oh good,' Helios said. 'I so hoped you'd say that. You won't mind popping over to the Stables of the Sun for an hour or so, then, and mending one of my celestial horses? Poor Abraxas has gone dreadfully lame, you see. Stepped on a sharp bit of star, or something. I'm sure that magical silver box of yours can fix him in two shakes of a comet's tail, though. Why don't you run along and fetch it, and then we'll be off? Quick as you like, now. I'll be waiting.'

Demon had no choice, but as he ran back

70

towards where he'd left the hippocamps, his mind was racing frantically. What if the box hadn't got here yet? What if he couldn't cure Helios's horses without it? Even worse, what if Poseidon found out he was working for his rival? 'I'm doomed,' he groaned as he ran into the stables, heart thumping like a mad maenad's drum. 'Doomed.'

'Why are you doomed?' asked a familiar high little voice. 'What's happened now?'

'Oh, Eunice,' he said miserably, slumping down on to one of the sleds, which, he was thankful to see, had now arrived from the undersea palace. 'I don't know what to do.' Eunice came to perch beside him as he explained.

'Well,' she said, tapping one small, pearly tooth with a sharp fingernail. 'I don't see what harm it can do if you just go for an hour or two. Cure Helios's horse and come straight back. Poseidon need never know – he and Queen Amphitrite are busy arranging all the stuff for the big party, anyway. I'll start the unpacking and look after the hippocamps, don't worry.'

Just then, there was a muffled squawk from behind them. Demon turned round. There was the box, wriggling in its seaweed bonds, and flashing an angry red.

'Implementing emergency escape mode,' it said, as several pairs of sharp scissors squeezed out from under its lid and started snipping away at both the kelp ropes and its waterproof cover.

Demon smiled gratefully at Eunice. 'Thanks,' he said. 'You're a . . . a . . . real starfish. I'll be back as soon as I can.' Now that he had the box, he was sure he really could cure Helios's horse – maybe things would be all right.

'Hello, box,' he said, helping it unravel itself completely and lifting it into his arms as soon as the scissors had retracted. 'Come on, we've got work to do.' The medical box uttered a cross metallic snarl as Demon ran, bobbing and bumping over the short springy grass towards the god of the sun. He sighed. It was clearly in a temper again.

Demon stumbled through Helios's door in the air at the god's heels. It felt like being bathed in warm spring sunshine – very different to the damp chilliness of the sea-palaces. On the other side was a gleaming stable block. Its roof was held up on towering ivory columns scattered with glittering flakes of gold; the walls were built of fire-coloured marble, and the door to each stall was marked with a big bronze flame. Beside it, a big, flat pasture filled with waving grass and flocks of silvery sheep and goats stretched as far as the eye could see. A truly massive golden chariot was parked by one of the many open barns, and six huge horses had their heads down in the meadow nearby, grazing hungrily, as nymphs bathed their sweaty sides with water from crystal basins.

'Hey, Petia,' called Helios. 'Bring Abraxas over here, will you.'

One of the nymphs set down her basin, and led her charge towards Demon and the sun god. Demon could see the enormous stallion limping badly.

'Oh dear,' he said. 'That must hurt.'

'It does,' whinnied Abraxas pitifully. 'A lot.'

'Put him in a stall,' Helios commanded. 'I just need to have another quick word with young Pandemonius here, and then I must go and see what my son Phaeton's been up to.' He chuckled, smiling his scary smile again. 'Naughty little scamp's always in trouble – why, he even tried to drive my chariot the other day before I caught him.'

Demon smiled back a bit nervously. What did Helios want now?

The god gripped him by the elbow again and bent in close. 'How are my friends the Cattle of the Sun doing?' the god asked unexpectedly. 'Enjoying the nice bales of hay I send from my fields, are they? Free of stomach gas? Keeping the goddesses happy at the lack of SMELL?'

'Y-y-yes, Your Sparkling Sunniness, th-th-they're f-fine,' Demon stammered, wondering what in Zeus's underpants the Cattle of the Sun had to do with anything. He soon found out.

'Glad to hear it,' said Helios. 'Now here's the thing. I might find I have a bit of a problem supplying hay to Olympus if, say, I heard that old Fish Father's hippocamps were in tip-top condition for the race. On the other hand, if I heard that they'd had a recurrence of that nasty scale condition – been slowed down a bit by it, if you get my meaning – then I might find that the lack of hay problem disappeared.' His grip tightened, and he swung Demon round to face him, piercing him with a bright golden glare. 'You understand me, young stable boy?'

As the god let him go and strode off round the corner of the Stables of the Sun, followed by the nymphs, Demon thought he understood only too well. It didn't matter what he did now – whichever god won, he was either fated to be turned into a Demon-sized smoking pile of charcoal by goddesses complaining about the terrible pong of gas coming from the stinky cows' bellies, or doomed to spend the next hundred years scrubbing salt off seaweed.

# 7
# DEMON'S DREADFUL DILEMMA

Demon's feet dragged as he walked slowly towards the lame Abraxas. Petia the nymph had left with her sisters, and he was alone with the enormous stallion. 'What am I going to do, box?' he asked it quietly. The box whirred and flashed blue.

'Random enquiry matrix not enabled,' said the box in its normal tinny tones. 'Questions of a medical nature only accepted at the present time.'

'Fat lot of help you are,' Demon growled as he

flipped the catch on the stall and went in. Bending down, he dumped the box on the golden straw and put his hand on Abraxas's lame leg. It was very hot, and the fetlock had swollen up. 'Help me with a cure for this, then,' he said crossly. The box clicked and whirred, as blue symbols flashed on its lid, and then it shot open with a clang, making the stallion back up nervously, half rearing. Demon only just rolled out of the way as a pair of enormous gold-shod hooves clattered past his face.

'Whoa! Whoa!' he said in his most soothing voice, grabbing at the stallion's halter. 'Calm down, Abraxas. It's only my silly old box having a look at your poorly foot. It didn't mean to scare you.'

'Well, it did,' whinnied a horsey voice high above his head. 'Nasty blue thing. I shall kick it if it does it again.'

The box scuttled out of the way like a crab, hurriedly dumping a bowl, a pair of tweezers, a big bunch of green bandages and a large packet of what looked like pink mud at Demon's feet.

'Analysis implemented. Foreign stellar object

detected in equine subject. Initiate interactive solution immediately,' it said in a snarky metallic gabble. Then it squeezed out of the stall and shut itself down in a sulk. Luckily Demon had been with the box long enough to understand its strange language.

'You've got a bit of star stuck in your foot, I think,' he said, picking up the huge hoof to inspect the soft part underneath. Sure enough, there was something sparkling caught there in its frog. Working quickly, he pulled the dazzling fragment of star out gently with the tweezers, then put a pink mud poultice on the sore bit before winding some of the cooling green bandages round the hot fetlock. A large soft muzzle snorted fragrant hay-scented air down the neck of his tunic.

'Thank you, Demon,' Abraxas snuffled. 'That feels much better. I must have stepped on a pointy bit of the Milky Way by mistake. Now I shall be able to race perfectly against Poseidon's hippocamps.'

Demon sighed. He'd forgotten about the race for a second.

As Demon led Abraxas slowly into his pasture, the other horses all crowded round.

'We've heard good things about you from our friends the pegasi!' they neighed. 'Keith says you're the best stable boy they've ever had! Can't you come and live with us for a bit? It's boring having no one but the nymphs to talk to. No one ever comes to visit us here – all we ever get to do is pull the sun across the sky, and that's hard work!'

Demon smiled. 'I'd love to,' he said, 'but the gods keep me very busy, you know, and I've got to get back to Poseidon's stables soon.' His face fell as he thought about his problem. 'And now your master has asked me to do something awful to the hippocamps.'

'What? What?' they whinnied. So Demon explained.

'If I make the hippocamps ill again, well . . . I'll . . . I'll be as bad as that horrible Heracles, hurting poor innocent beasts!' he finished despairingly as the huge horses began to swish their tails angrily.

'Helios can't make you do that,' they neighed. 'Making beasts sick is wrong.'

'I KNOW!' Demon groaned, running his hands through his curly hair so it went all sticky-uppy. 'But how do I get out of it?'

The horses went into a huddle, whickering softly to one another. Then Abraxas raised his head.

'We'll help you stand up to our master, Demon,' he whinnied. 'But you'll have to be clever. You'll have to trick a god, and so will we.'

'I can be clever,' said Demon, crossing his fingers that he could – and that he wouldn't be caught. He didn't even hesitate. Hurting any beast was totally against his nature – he just couldn't do it. If it meant tricking a god, then . . . well, he would, and to Hades with the consequences.

As Abraxas explained the plan quietly, his whiskery muzzle tickling Demon's ear, he began to feel a bit more hopeful. Maybe this could work. By the time Helios came striding across the pasture, Demon knew exactly what he had to do. He walked forward to meet the sun god, with the six white horses making a solid, comforting line behind him.

'What's this?' said Helios. 'You horses all look very serious for this time of night!' The god frowned, hot, bright sun sparks erupting from the rays of his crown. 'And so do you, young Pandemonius.' Demon took a deep breath. Maybe it would be his last if Helios didn't buy his story. But he just didn't care. He'd do what was right even if he did end up as a pile of ash.

'Well, it's like this, Your Solar Godnificence,' he said in a rush. 'Me and your horses don't think I should do what you asked me to do to Poseidon's hippocamps. M-my job is making beasts well, not ill. Poseidon would suspect your involvement immediately. B-b-but I think m-maybe I can help you win in another way.' He stepped backwards into the line of horses and crossed his fingers tightly, praying that Helios wouldn't hear the lie in his voice.

But Helios was looking at his horses.

'Well, my celestial steeds!' he snarled. 'And you

support this wretched stable boy? What will you do if I say no to this son of Pan?'

'Then the sun's chariot will not run across the sky till you agree,' neighed all six horses together.

'So! Even you betray me!' shouted the sun god angrily.

There was a sudden blast of heat, and Demon smelled burning as the edges of his chiton begin to crisp and smoulder. He began to talk very fast.

'There's a magic herb,' he gabbled, batting at the sparks frantically. 'It makes beasts run faster than the North Wind if you paint the juice of it on their hooves. I-I can get it for you.'

Helios grabbed him and lifted him up by the front of his tunic, leaving his bare legs kicking and dangling.

'What is this herb?' he growled. 'I've never heard of such a thing.'

'I-i-it's c-called g-gorgos anemos, and it c-comes from the kingdom of the Old Man of the Sea,' Demon stammered. Helios threw him down in the grass.

'Very well,' he growled. 'But mark me well, stable boy. If my horses don't run faster than light itself in that race, I will personally see to it that you are set as a spot in the heart of the sun to burn for all eternity!' With that, Helios opened another door in the air and shoved Demon through it to Poseidon's island, throwing the medical box after him.

Demon gulped and gasped, scrambling and stumbling back down the narrow, rocky path to the stables. The first part of the plan had worked. Now he just had to persuade Eunice to help him with the second, but it would have to wait till the morning. He was too tired to do anything but lie down on his pallet in the cave roof and go to sleep.

A strong smell of seaweed met him as he woke up the next morning. Stretching and yawning, he rolled out of bed and dived down into the stables. The hippocamps all had their noses buried in their mangers. As he swam up again, he saw Eunice perched on a rock above him, playing a little flute crusted with shells.

'Goodness,' she gasped, dropping it with a crunch. 'Whatever happened to your chiton?' Demon glanced down. There *were* a few big burn holes in it, and some finger-shaped scorch marks. He could see them even through the water.

'Helios got a bit angry with me,' he said. 'I've sort of played a trick on him, and I need you to help me with the next bit of it.'

Eunice turned pale green. 'Me?' she asked nervously. 'A trick on Helios? Why me? What can I do?'

'Well,' he said, taking a deep breath and hoping. 'Do you by any chance know where the Old Man of the Sea lives?'

Eunice did the last thing he expected. She laughed.

'Well, of course I do, silly,' she giggled. 'He's my dad.'

Demon goggled at her. 'But . . . but . . . I thought your father was called Nereus!'

'He is. But because he's so ancient and wise, lots of people call him the Old Man of the Sea too. What do you need him for?'

'Helios's horses told me that a magic herb called gorgos anemos grows in his kingdom, and I need it for my trick to work.'

Eunice's mouth fell open in shock.

'Gorgos anemos?' Eunice shrieked. 'B-but that's our swiftweed flower. No one's supposed to know about that but my family. NO ONE! How did those wretched celestial horses find out about it, by Hades' toenails?' She dived off the rock and swam over to him. 'I think you'd better tell me all about this trick you've come up with at ONCE,' she said.

So Demon explained about how Helios had wanted him to sabotage the hippocamps, and how he and the horses had come up with a brilliant plan to trick the sun god instead.

'The horses want it to be a fair race with no cheating,' he explained. 'So although I'm going to paint their hooves with the magic liquid so they do what Helios wants and gallop faster than ever before, I'm also going to put it on the hippocamps' hooves and flippers – only Helios won't know that. So I won't have to make the hippocamps ill again, and whichever god wins will really truly have the proper fastest team.'

'It's still very dangerous,' said Eunice. 'What if Helios finds out about our family secret? Even worse, if he loses, he's bound to be furious anyway and turn you into a sunspot like he said he would.'

Demon thought it was best not to mention at this point that he'd already told Helios about the magic herb – well, how was *he* to have known it was a secret?

'The thing is,' he said instead, 'Zeus will be at the race, and everyone knows he hates cheating. If Helios loses and comes after me, the horses have promised to threaten him with Zeus's wrath. I-I just have to take the risk. It's only a stupid race, and I won't hurt a beast deliberately, not for any god!'

Eunice sighed. 'All right, then. Let's hitch up

the hippocamps and find my dad,' she said. 'Though if he ever finds out that I'm using swiftweed for anyone other than family, I'll probably be shut in a cave for a million years and have to marry the Giant Squid.'

# 8

# THE OLD MAN
# OF THE SEA

Demon and Eunice harnessed all nine hippocamps to the chariot. Going to visit Eunice's dad was the perfect excuse to exercise them, just as Poseidon had instructed.

They squashed in, one behind the other, and with Demon at the reins they shot out of the stables and into the open air, splishing and sploshing over the crests of the waves. It was very strange being in the driving seat, but Demon soon got used to it, though he didn't dare go as fast as Poseidon.

'Which way?' Demon yelled, spitting out a mouthful of seawater.

'Straight on!' Eunice yelled over his shoulder, her dark green hair flying in the breeze. Soon Demon began to enjoy himself, and as he got more confident they went faster and faster, zipping past islands, racing dolphins and sea-skimming seagulls. Then, just as they reached two huge red spires of rock sticking up out of the ocean, Eunice shouted, 'Dive!'

This time, Demon hardly noticed the change from air to water as the hippocamps shot downwards, then levelled out and began cantering along a white, sandy road at the bottom of the sea. He was too busy holding on to the mass of reins, keeping the chariot straight, and looking out of the corners of his eyes at the place he was riding through. A tall green forest of kelp trees surrounded them, trunks wavering in the current, with colourful rippling anemones set in clumps at their roots. Small seahorses, like living jewels, flitted through the branches like birds, and came to perch on Demon's head and shoulders, making tiny shrill squeaks of joy. Then the forest thinned, turning into a series of large meadows of seagrass where herds of strange-looking sea monsters with hairy nostrils, crayfish tails and rows of neat webbed feet were grazing. As he was wondering what they were, Demon saw a large cave-mouth ahead.

'That's my dad's house,' said Eunice. 'Drive up to the front – we can tether the chariot there.'

'What should I say?' he asked.

'Leave it to me,' said Eunice. 'My dad can be a bit funny sometimes. The only thing you have to remember is never to accept his challenge to a wrestling contest. He always wins – and he always cheats!' Demon would like to have heard more, but Eunice was already slipping out of the chariot and tying the hippocamps up to a barnacle-encrusted ring set in the rock outside the cave.

'Stay there!' Demon said to them sternly, as he

scrambled out after her. The hippocamps looked at him sideways out of their blue eyes, put their heads down and started tearing up seagrass.

'Hey, Dad! Where are you? It's me, Eunice! I've brought a friend to visit,' she called, swimming into the cave. Demon followed her. The cave was dimly lit by a series of angler fish set in niches in the walls. It had a far more homely feel than Poseidon's palace, with bits of wrecked ship serving as chairs and tables, and some rather rickety shell ornaments which had clearly been made by Eunice and her sisters dotted about the floor and on the driftwood shelves.

'In here,' came a booming voice.

'This way,' Eunice hissed, beckoning Demon into a smaller cave. Stooped over a pile of black horned objects was the Old Man of the Sea. His long white hair was tied back with a string of bladderwrack, and his beard was knotted with shells and small starfish. In his hand he had a large needle, threaded with an array of sparkling jewels. Eunice grinned.

'Decorating purses for the mermaids again, Dad?' she asked.

Nereus grunted. 'Careless girls are always losing 'em,' he said. 'I never have enough in stock.' He looked up at Demon. 'Who's this, then? Some young whippersnapper come to challenge me, I suppose.'

'No! Of course not, Dad. This is Demon, Pan's son. He's looking after Poseidon's hippocamps for now, but he's really the Official Beastkeeper on Olympus.' Nereus looked at Demon from under bushy white eyebrows.

'You sure you don't want to wrestle me, son?'

Demon shook his head, remembering what Eunice had told him.

'Not really, thank you very much, Your Ancientness. I'm a bit short for it.'

'Well, you're no Heracles, that's for sure. Wretched heroes — I hate 'em. Always wanting something for nothing. Suppose you want something too, do you?'

Demon was about to answer, when Eunice trod hard on his toe with one of her flipper feet.

'No no,' she said airily. 'Demon just wanted to see where I used to live. We were exercising the hippocamps and thought we'd drop by and visit. But now you mention it, I could do with a bit of swiftweed juice for my dolphin. Poor old Seapetal's fins are getting a bit creaky, and we can't keep up with my sisters any more, so I want to rub some on him before we go for our next ride.' She beamed up at him lovingly. 'I know you don't give it out to just anybody, but I am your favourite daughter, after all!'

Nereus stared at her suspiciously.

'Swiftweed juice, eh? Dangerous stuff, that. You be careful with it. Use a seagull-feather brush to put it on like I taught you, and don't use too much, or the poor beast will take off like a rocket.' He glared ferociously at Demon. 'And don't you go telling anyone about it, either, young Demon. It's meant to be a family secret, that juice is, and Eunice here had no business talking about it in front of you. If that wretched Heracles or any of the other heroes gets to hear about it, I'll have them tromping down here in droves, wanting some to make their stupid arrows fly faster, or something.'

'Don't worry, I'd never tell anyone. I don't like Heracles either,' said Demon. 'He's always bashing up my beasts.'

'Well, see that you don't. Or I'll get Poseidon to hang you up by your toes for the telchines to nibble on.' The Old Man of the Sea moved across to a large alcove set in the rock, and picked up a crystal jug full of bright orange liquid.

'Here,' said Eunice, pulling out a large bottle with a carved stone stopper from inside her robe and handing it to him. 'You can put it in this.' She reached up and gave him a kiss on his hairy cheek. 'Thanks, you're the best dad in the world.'

'You and your little tricks,' he chuckled, handing her the filled bottle. 'Now get away with you, child, and give my love to your sisters. Tell them to come and visit soon. Amphitrite keeps all of you too busy!'

'I will,' said Eunice, pulling Demon out of the cave and towards the tethered hippocamps. 'I promise.' She put her finger to her lips as soon as they were round the corner and out of sight. 'Don't say anything – the walls have ears,' she whispered, nodding towards the angler-fish lights.

Eunice slipped out of the chariot as soon as they drove into the palace stables. 'I'd better go and check on Amphitrite. She said I still had to do my duties for her even if I was helping you in my spare time. I'll be down again as quick as I can – sorry to leave you with all the work.' Fumbling in the pocket of her robe, she thrust the bottle of swiftweed juice at him. 'Hide this in a safe place, and DON'T use it till I can show you how.' Then she shot off before he could say a single word.

Demon shoved the bottle under a bale of silver seaweed as the hippocamps began to prance and dance with impatience to get to their mangers. He'd deal with it later.

Seeing to the hippocamps and cleaning the harness took a good long while, but Demon felt a bit lonely once he'd finished. The hippocamps weren't very good company – they only spoke in single words, and he missed Arnie the griffin's snarky chat. He got out the bottle of swiftweed juice and looked over at the box, which was still on the high rocky shelf where he'd left it.

'Box,' he said politely. 'Would you mind keeping this safe for me? It's pretty dangerous stuff, apparently, and I need to make sure that nobody but me or Eunice uses it.'

The silver box shuddered and let out a couple of blue sparks, but eventually its lid opened with a cross-sounding creak. 'Insert object,' it said, rather grudgingly. Demon placed the bottle inside, and immediately the lid snapped shut. The box began to hum busily. 'Poison protocols in process,' it announced, just as a flashing red skull and crossbones appeared on each of its sides. Demon patted it, then yelped as a strange tingly shock passed through his hand.

'Ouch!' he yelled.

The box glowed rather smugly.

'Safety procedures present and correct,' it said. 'Item now password protected.'

'Password?' asked Demon angrily, sucking his sore fingers. 'What's a password?'

'Mother's name plus father's gift,' it whirred.

Demon thought for a moment, puzzled. Then it suddenly came to him.

'Er, that would be . . . er . . . Carys and pan pipes,' he said.

'Correct. Do you wish to retrieve item?'

'No, not now. You keep it safe. Thanks, box. You're the best.'

The box glowed bright blue with pleasure.

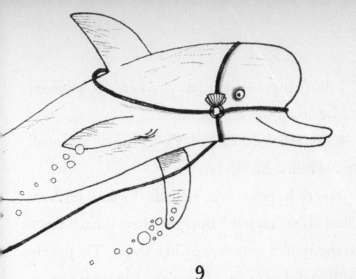

# 9

# THE SWIFTWEED TEST

The stables were spick and span, the hippocamps were happy, healthy, polished, exercised and fed. Demon wondered what to do next. He wasn't used to having only one set of beasts to look after. Should he try to find Eunice? Should he report to Poseidon? Or should he find the kitchens? Since he was now hungrier than a pack of ravening sharks and his stomach was in danger of sticking to his spine, he decided that finding the kitchens was pretty urgent.

'I don't suppose you know where the kitchens are?' he asked the hippocamps.

'KITCHENS! FOOD! YUM!' they squealed. Demon rolled his eyes.

'You're hopeless,' he sighed. 'I guess I'll have to find them myself.' But just then Eunice came into the stables with five of her sisters. They were all riding dolphins, and Eunice had another one on a silver rein.

'Come on, Demon,' she called. 'I've brought Seawhistle for you to ride. Amphitrite wants us to collect some shells for decorating the banqueting hall. There's a perfect beach on the island next door.' Unfortunately, Demon's stomach gave an enormous gurgle right as she stopped talking, and the nereids all giggled.

'I think he's hungry,' said the one in the pink robe.

'Poor boy,' said the one in yellow. 'Haven't you been feeding him, Eunice?'

Demon felt his face getting redder than the setting sun as he climbed onto Seawhistle's back.

'I can feed myself perfectly well!' he snapped, wriggling himself into place behind the big back fin. 'It's just that I haven't quite found out where the kitchens are yet.'

Eunice laughed.

'Well, that's easy enough,' she said. 'Let's go there before we start on the shells. I'm starving too, now I come to think of it.'

The palace kitchens were amazing. Pots and pans full of delicious-looking things bounced and boiled on top of jets of scalding water, and piles of strange sea vegetables were being chopped and shaped and stuffed, along with endless baskets of shellfish. There was even a huge jelly castle being decorated with edible shells and strands of seaweed. Poseidon's cooks seemed to be preparing enough food to feed a thousand gods and goddesses and Demon's stomach was soon as full as it could hold. Soon afterwards, he found himself collecting shells on a little white, sandy beach. The nereids thought it was funny to pelt him with wet seaweed, but he soon got his own back by stuffing sand down the back of their robes.

After the first day, Demon quickly fell into a routine. What with exercising the hippocamps in the morning, getting them ready for Poseidon's daily inspection, then taking time off in the afternoons to ride Seawhistle and explore with Eunice and the other nereids, the days before the race soon passed. Despite what Eunice said about her sisters, they were fun to be with, always laughing and playing jokes as they showed him around the palace, challenging him to swimming races (which he always lost), and generally treating him like a long-lost younger brother. But the night before the race he started to get nervous again. Every time he thought of how much could go wrong, he got a nasty sinking feeling of doom in his stomach.

As he was giving the hippocamps their last feed of the night, he was surprised to see Eunice ride in on her dolphin, Seapetal, with Seawhistle swimming behind her. By that time he had rumpled his hair into a tangled bird's nest with worry. He was convinced the whole plan was going to end in disaster.

'What are you doing here?' he asked, as nasty wriggly-worry things joined the doom feeling. 'I-i-is something wrong?'

'No, nothing's *wrong*, except that my sisters are all fluffing and faffing and looking at stupid jewels,' she said crossly. 'Luckily Amphitrite is too busy choosing which dress to wear tomorrow to notice I'm not there, so I thought I'd escape. Want to take Seawhistle for a night ride? There's a lovely full moon, and the stars are much brighter than Halia's silly old opals.' Then she frowned, looking at him. 'What's the matter, Demon? Why is your hair all sticky-uppy like that?'

'What if the swiftweed juice doesn't work?' he burst out. 'What if it's a bad batch or something? What if Poseidon and Helios find out? What if the effect runs out halfway through the race . . .' Eunice rode over and grabbed his shoulder, giving him a little shake.

'You big silly,' she said. 'Of course it'll work – it lasts for a whole day usually. And I'll be there to help with the hippocamps. You'll see, it'll all be fine. But if you're really worried, we can try out a tiny drop on Seapetal and Seawhistle here. They won't tell anyone, will you?' The dolphins opened their mouths and grinned, shaking their heads violently.

'Race you,' they whistled to each other. 'Last one back's a barnacle's bottom!'

Eunice was very impressed with the box's security measures. 'It's better than a whole legion of those stupid Triton guards,' she said as Demon spoke the password and the bottle of swiftweed appeared. The box glowed with pleasure again. Taking a tiny seagull-feather brush from her pocket, she dipped just the very tip into the bottle, and painted a minuscule amount on the dolphins' front flippers and their tails, before putting everything back in the box.

'Now,' she said, jumping on to Seapetal's back, 'let's race!'

Demon hardly had time to scramble on to Seawhistle before Eunice and Seapetal shot out of the stables faster than Zeus's lightning bolts.

Seawhistle followed, streaking past his friend as Demon clung on for dear life. Right out into the ocean they raced, following the silvery path of the full moon. The stars zipped past in a blur overhead, as the dolphins whistled and clicked with glee, overtaking shoals of very surprised-looking fish and jumping high in the air. By the time they turned back, Demon had no more worries about whether the swiftweed would work or not. It was brilliant stuff! But as they came in sight of the palace, they saw an extraordinary sight in the night sky. An arch of rainbow-coloured light streamed down from the moonlit heavens, and into the palace, lighting up the sky. Demon reined Seawhistle to a halt, Eunice slowing beside him.

'Whatever is THAT?' asked Eunice, shading her eyes.

'Gods!' Seawhistle whistled, dancing among the waves.

'Goddesses!' clicked Seapetal. 'Lots of them.'

'Yes,' said Demon, recognising it. 'It's the Iris

Express from Olympus. The gods all use it for travelling between there and earth. I'd better start getting the hippocamps ready. Poseidon will be coming to get the chariot soon.' He gulped. 'I-I just hope Helios doesn't arrive at the same time.'

'Oh no!' gasped Eunice. 'I've got to get back to the queen. If the gods and goddesses are arriving already, Amphitrite will definitely notice if I'm not there. She's bound to be fussing that Aphrodite has a better dress for the feast or something stupid. Come on, Seapetal, quick! I'll see you later, Demon – and DON'T WORRY!'

Her voice faded into the distance as Demon headed more slowly to the stables. Soon it would be dawn, and the race would begin.

Even though Demon now knew that the swiftweed worked, he was still nervous. To keep himself occupied, he polished the sleepy hippocamps over and over till their bronze scales shone. Even the fiercest one was used to him now, and it nuzzled his pockets for the purple sea-berry treats he'd taken to bringing them from the kitchen. Just as he was going to get the harness out ready, there was a blaze of light in the cave entrance.

'Time to keep your promise, stable boy,' Helios said, appearing through his door in the air and smiling his dangerously white smile. 'I do hope you succeeded in getting what you needed from the Old Man of the Sea. It would be such a shame to turn you into a sunspot when it seems you've worked so hard polishing up those stupid sea steeds for his Foolish Fishiness.' He smirked nastily. 'Shiny scales won't help them go faster, though, will they?'

'N-no, Your Sunshiny Superbness. They definitely won't.' It wasn't a lie, Demon thought. Shininess *wouldn't* help the hippocamps go faster. 'I-I'll just go g-g-get the magic juice.'

Taking a deep breath to calm himself, he whispered the password to the box, got the swiftweed juice out and put it safely inside his robe, together with the seagull-feather paintbrush. 'Ready,' he said, scrambling up on to the rock, hoping that Poseidon wouldn't come to the stables and find him gone. Helios grabbed his hand and pulled him through the door to the sun-drenched other side. Waiting just outside their pasture were the six golden-maned celestial horses, each with a nymph at its head. They were already harnessed to the gigantic Chariot of the Sun, which had a long, braided rope snaking out behind it into the distance. Demon could see the top of a shining golden ball just poking over the horizon.

'Hurry up, boy,' snapped Helios. 'Eos of the Dawn waits for no god – and she'll be going to the starting line soon.' He seemed nervous, but not as nervous as Demon, whose hands were shaking as he brushed each shining golden hoof with a drop of swiftweed juice. Abraxas bent his head and brushed Demon comfortingly with his white muzzle, but he didn't say anything. It was too dangerous with Helios so near. Finally Demon finished and stood up. The horses were now pawing restlessly at the ground, their skins rippling and shuddering.

'All done, Your Celestial Cloudlessness,' he said, stuffing the bottle and brush back into his chiton. Helios stepped forward, leaning over him until they were nearly nose to nose. Demon could feel the heat of the sun god's gaze singeing his eyebrows, but he didn't dare move.

'And can you swear to me that they'll run faster than they ever have before, stable boy?' the sun god asked softly, his voice as menacing as the Giant Scorpion's sting.

'Y-y-yes,' Demon stammered. 'Faster than the North and South Winds together, I swear. You'll notice the difference in them immediately.' He just hoped the hippocamps would run equally as fast.

'They'd better, or you'll be a crispy sunspot by sundown!' With one last threatening glare, Helios pushed Demon back through the door in the air and into the hippocamp stables, where he fell into the water with a splash. The blaze of light clicked out as suddenly as it had appeared.

'I wish his own sun would burn him up to a crisp,' muttered Demon angrily, paddling towards a rock. 'I'm fed up with gods pushing me around and bullying me.' He went to get the harness in a very grumpy mood.

## 10

# THE RACE OF SEA AND SUN

As Demon finished polishing the very last buckle, Poseidon whirled into the cave, golden trident in hand, his black beard bristling and crackling with purple energy.

'Good, good,' he said. 'Glad to see you've got everything in tip-top condition early, Pandemonius. We don't want to be outshone by those celestial nags, do we?' Demon shook his head.

'Definitely not, Your Marine Magnificence,' he said.

'You can harness them up and bring the chariot round to the east side of the island now. Eos is going to start the race just as dawn breaks. We're going to show that stupid sun boy show-off who's fastest, aren't we, my lovelies?' said the sea god, as he visited each hippocamp's stall and murmured words of encouragement.

'GO FAST! FAST! FAST! FAST!' they trumpeted, beginning to rear and plunge.

'Calm down, calm down! Save your energy for the race!' Poseidon boomed, patting Demon on the shoulder. 'I'll see you there, stable boy. Now I've got to go and greet my fellow gods.' He pulled a face. 'Not my kind of thing, but Amphitrite insists we do things properly. Says Olympus will look down on us if we don't.' With that, he disappeared in a sparkling whoosh of seawater.

Should he put the swiftweed juice on the hippocamps now, Demon wondered. No. That wouldn't do at all. Helios was bound to think it was suspicious if they galloped up to the starting line too fast. He'd have to sneak it on at the last minute without Helios seeing. His heart began to thunder like a whole herd of centaurs. However was he going to pull this off?

He harnessed the excited hippocamps to the chariot with trembling fingers, then got in and headed for the east side of the island. Driving up on to a shallow beach in the grey light before the dawn, he jumped out and stood ready by the hippocamps' heads. Up on the cliff above a huge crowd of gods and goddesses had gathered, seated on a bank of chairs covered in silken cushions. Craning his neck, he spotted Zeus's crown of lightning bolts – and was that Hera beside him, waving a fan of peacock feathers and talking to Poseidon and Amphitrite? He scuttled round to the other side of the hippocamps. He didn't want *her* spotting him! Then he noticed something else. Making her way down the cliff path was a tall goddess dressed in palest pink. Eos, Goddess of the Dawn, was on her way to start the race. He looked around him frantically. Where was Eunice? He couldn't do this without her help, and time was running out!

Luckily, just then, a breathless Eunice swam up on Seapetal. 'Have you put it on them?' she hissed at him as she slid off the dolphin's back.

'No,' said Demon. 'Helios's horses are done, but I haven't had a chance to do the hippocamps yet. I was waiting for you. Quick! Hold them while I pretend to inspect their hooves and tails.' Working fast, and keeping a nervous eye out for Helios and his chariot, Demon daubed a drop of swiftweed juice on each hippocamp tail, fin and hoof. Just as he'd finished the last one, he saw Poseidon striding towards him across the sand. He shoved the bottle and brush back into his chiton as the hippocamps beside him started to act even more like high-strung thoroughbreds than usual. Their front hooves were pawing at the sand, and their tails thrashing the water behind, making the chariot toss and sway in the waves. The swiftweed was definitely taking effect! Demon held the chariot steady as Poseidon climbed in, and the god nodded in thanks as he took up the reins.

'Whoa!' he yelled as the hippocamps plunged and reared with impatience to be off. 'Whoa, you eager beasties!' He waved frantically to Eos as a tiny rim of light appeared on the eastern horizon, six white horses silhouetted against its brightness. Helios had arrived!

'Ready when you are, Sun Dragger,' he shouted, his voice booming across the waves as he raised his trident. 'I can hardly hold mine back – you don't have a chance with those celestial donkeys of yours!'

The sun god laughed rudely. 'Eat my spray, Fish Father!' he yelled back, cracking his starry whip so that his horses reared in their traces.

'On your marks,' shouted Eos, raising her arms in the air. 'Get set! GO!' Out of her fingers shot beams of pink radiance, which lit up the whole sky. The hippocamps hurtled forward in a froth of foam, and Helios's team streaked away in the distance. Within seconds they were out of sight over the horizon, roared on by the crowd of gods and goddesses on the hill above the shore, and a cheering mass of sea folk bobbing in the waves. The race was on!

'Let's go and find my sisters,' said Eunice. 'You can't do anything more now, and we might be able to see better from up there.' Together, they climbed the little path up the cliff, Eunice stumbling a bit on her flipper feet. Demon grabbed her arm as she nearly tripped on a rock.

'Oops!' she said, wincing. 'I'm not really used to walking on this stony stuff. It feels like knives digging into me.'

Demon hadn't really thought about that.

'Do you want a ride?' he asked.

'Yes, please!' she said gratefully. So Demon carried her up the cliff on his back, wheezing and panting. She was a lot more solid than she looked, and he was quite glad to set her down on the soft grass at the top. Squeezing past a mass of nymphs and fauns who were chattering and shoving each other, and standing on tiptoe to see something just in front of them, they came out by the crowd of seated gods and goddesses. Zeus was standing on a disc of air in front of them, his hands creating what looked like a picture in the air. It was a huge revolving blue globe, with white at the top and bottom, and lots of large, green strangely-shaped blobs set in the blue bits. Two fiery dots – one gold, one silver – were moving across it, leaving trails behind them. The gold dot was slightly in front of the silver one, and the two trails led back to one flashing red beacon. All the gods and goddesses were yelling for their favourites.

'Come on, Poseidon,' shouted a deep voice just above Demon's head. He looked up and saw a familiar figure with a black beard and a dirty face. It was his friend Hephaestus! He reached up and tugged on the blacksmith god's robe.

'Hello, Heffy,' he called. Hephaestus looked down, frowning, but when he saw Demon his soot-stained face broke into a broad grin.

'Well, if it isn't young Pandemonius,' he said. 'What are you doing down here, you cheeky brat?

And who's your friend?' Demon introduced Eunice, who smiled nervously.

'Ah, one of the nereids, are you?' said the blacksmith god, nodding his head wisely. Then he turned back to Demon, a stern look on his face. 'There's been an awful lot of noise coming from the stables lately, young man – you should keep those beasts of yours under better control.'

'I haven't been there,' Demon said, hastily explaining about Poseidon and the hippocamps. 'Hermes was supposed to send someone called Autolycus to look after the beasts while I was away.' He looked worried. 'Maybe he hasn't been looking after them properly. Er, there hasn't been a smell of . . . you know . . . has there?'

'What, poo? Not that I've noticed,' said Hephaestus. He looked over at Zeus's picture. 'Come ON, Poseidon,' he roared, shaking his fist in the air.

'Er, excuse me, Your Godnificence,' said Eunice timidly. 'What *is* that round thing?'

'That? Why that's a picture of the whole world,

of course, sea child.' He pointed to the two moving dots. 'There's Poseidon, see? He's the silver dot. And there's Helios – he's the gold dot. Where we are now is the red dot – the start and finish line. Zeus is judging the race, you know – and this way we can all see there's no cheating.' Hephaestus cleared his throat and looked round, lowering his voice slightly. 'I've wagered Ares one of my magic suits of armour that Poseidon will win. He's supporting Helios, of course, but I reckon Poseidon has the edge. Helios's horses are ahead right now, but they've got that heavy sun to pull, remember, and I think they'll be all out of juice by dusk.'

Demon said nothing, but he heaved a deep sigh. He was pretty much in trouble whichever god lost.

The lead changed several times throughout that long day. Finally, the silver and gold trails were almost at the red dot again, and, as the sun sank towards the west, the gods and goddesses cheered even louder, shaking the earth with their cries. Demon's heart began to pound in his chest. Helios's gold dot was just in front, but Poseidon's silver one was creeping up on him.

Suddenly, with a flash of light, the two teams burst into sight. Zeus raised his hand, and a flash of lightning sizzled and hissed as it hit the waves, laying out a long red finish line in front of the two teams of galloping steeds. Poseidon's trident streamed with purple fire, which whipped out over the hippocamps' heads, as Helios urged his horses on with a crack of starlight, and a burst of sun flame from his crown. Slowly, inch by inch, the hippocamps were catching up with the celestial horses, and Demon found his fists were clenched so hard that his fingernails dug painfully into his palms.

'Come on, come on, come ON,' he muttered as Eunice shrieked and danced beside him. With a last, mighty effort, the hippocamps drew level with their rivals, and as their noses touched the lightning line, two identical spears of red flame shot into the air beside each chariot.

Zeus's voice boomed out like thunder, as Helios

and Poseidon reined their steeds to a halt. 'I declare this race a DEAD HEAT!' he roared into a sudden silence. 'You have BOTH won!'

Poseidon and Helios began to laugh at the same time.

'Good contest, Sun Dragger!' said the sea god, reaching over and holding out his hand to his rival deity. 'My hippocamps ran the best race of their lives.'

'Yes, good race, Fish Father,' said Helios, stretching over and shaking Poseidon's hand firmly. 'The four winds themselves couldn't have beaten either of us today. My horses have NEVER run so fast.'

As Helios spoke, his eyes sought out Demon in the crowd, and, as the sun god gave him a nod, Demon felt a big burden of fear slip from his shoulders. He wouldn't be a sunspot or have to scrub seaweed after all!

# 11

# THE ORDER OF THE OCEAN

'Let us care for our gallant beasts,' said Poseidon, raising his trident, 'and then we will feast and salute each other's victory.'

Demon knew this was his signal. Running down the cliff path, he sprinted to the hippocamps' heads. Their sides were heaving, and they looked tired, but Demon could see they were happy.

'HOORAY! HOORAY! HOORAY!' they whinnied, as Helios and his horses finally pulled the sun beneath the horizon and dusk fell. Poseidon clapped him on the shoulder.

'Well done, stable boy,' he said. 'We didn't win, but we didn't lose either. I've never known them go so quick as they did today. Whatever you've been doing to them, it's certainly paid off.' He looked at Demon. 'Don't suppose I can persuade you to stay here and look after them full-time, can I?'

'Well, Your Mighty Marineness, I'd love to, really,' said Demon carefully, 'but I don't think Zeus would be very happy about it, and it wouldn't be fair on my poor beasts up on Olympus.'

'Well, I suppose not. But if they get sick again, I'll be calling on you – you can be sure of that. Now take these poor beasties back to their stalls and give them a good feed and a rub down. Then come back to the feast – you deserve a reward for all your hard work.'

'SEAWEED! SPONGE! SLEEP!' neighed the hippocamps eagerly, as they galloped round the island to their stable. Clearly the swiftweed hadn't worn off yet. Demon took care of them, and then made his way up to the banqueting hall, wiping the worst smears of sea-slug slime off his chiton as he went.

The banqueting hall at Macris was as magnificent as Poseidon's undersea throne room. The towering walls were banded with stripes of lapis lazuli and mother of pearl, and under the pale blue crystal ceiling sparkling yellow stars whirled and shone, speckling the room with twinkles of moving light. Water lapped around tall columns of white coral, and on a raised dais carved with sea creatures was an enormous shell-decorated silver table where the gods and goddesses were sitting. Smaller silver tables led down in a series of steps from its ends, eventually dipping down into the water so that the sea-folk could eat comfortably.

Demon looked around the noisy room, buzzing with chatter. Where should he sit? Then he spotted Eunice and her nereid sisters, waving and beckoning from a table just below the dais. 'Over here, Demon,' they called, so Demon made his way over, and sat down beside them.

'Look!' Eunice said, pointing to a bowl of golden-red fruit. 'Sun berries! Try one, they're delicious. Helios decided that as he was joint victor he'd bring half the feast from his kitchens. There's stuff here I've never eaten before, but it's all yummy!' Demon wasted no time in filling his plate. Eunice was right – it *was* all delicious.

The evening passed in a blur of eating and drinking, and just as Demon was stuffing in one last morsel of suncake, Poseidon banged on the floor with his trident. There was an earth-shaking boom, and the whole banqueting hall trembled.

'Brother Zeus,' he said loudly. 'I have borrowed your stable boy, and much as I should like to keep him, I must return him to Olympus. But first I would like to reward him. Stand forth, Pandemonius, son of Pan.'

Demon nearly choked.

'What, me?' he whispered to Eunice.

She gave him a little push.

'Yes, you! Go on, don't keep him waiting!'

Demon wriggled under the table and walked

up the steps, his sandals sloshing slightly and his chiton holey and grubby, to kneel in front of Poseidon's seat. He didn't dare look up with so many gods and goddesses staring at him.

'You have done me great service, son of Pan, and I hereby award you the Order of the Ocean, and the freedom of my seas.' Poseidon was holding out a large speckled cowrie shell with golden edges, hanging from a heavy golden chain. Demon scrambled off his knees and leaned forward, so the sea god could hang it round his neck.

'You may also ask a reward of me,' the sea god went on. 'Pandemonius, what reward can I give you? Jewels, pearls – perhaps some golden treasure?' Demon shook his head, speechless. He didn't need any of those things. Then he caught a glimpse of Eunice, and suddenly he knew exactly what he was going to ask.

'Well, Your Serene Saltiness, maybe there's one thing. C-could you possibly make my friend Eunice the official stable girl to the hippocamps? The Tritons don't seem that interested in looking after them, a-and Eunice is really very good with them and the d-dolphins, m-much better than she is at brushing hair.' Demon stopped abruptly, aware that he was babbling a bit.

Poseidon laughed. 'Very well,' he said. 'Come here, young Eunice. I can't say I'm very surprised after all the times Queen Amphitrite has complained about you running away to hang around my stables!'

Eunice came up to the dais, her smile as wide as an opened oystershell, and stopped by Demon's side.

'From this moment forward, Eunice the nereid is Official Handmaid to the Hippocamps and Damsel of the Dolphins,' Poseidon announced. The room erupted in loud claps and cheers around them as they made their way back to their table, where Eunice's sisters were clapping loudest of all.

'Thanks,' she whispered to Demon. 'A proper job at last! I'm so happy I could pop like a squashed sea slug!'

'Ugh! Gross!' he whispered back.

But he didn't really mean it. He was too happy himself. Tomorrow he'd go back to the stables on Olympus and sort out whatever mess Autolycus had made of them, but tonight . . . tonight he was going to celebrate his lucky escape from sunspots and seaweed scrubbing with Eunice and all his new nereid friends.

# GLOSSARY

## BEASTS:

**Basilisk** *(BASS-uh-lisk)*: King of the serpents. Every bit of him is pointy, poisonous, or perilous.

**Celestial Horses** *(SELL-ess-tee-ul)*: Giant white stallions with gold manes who pull Helios's chariot and the sun from east to west every day around the Earth.

**Cerberus** *(SER-ber-us)*: Huge three-headed, snake-maned hound, Guardian of the Underworld, and Hades' favourite cuddly pet.

**Chiron** *(KY-ron)*: A super-centaur – part horse, part man, with all the best parts of each.

**Cretan Bull** *(KREE-tun)*: A furious, fire-breathing bull. Don't stand too close.

**Griffin** *(GRIH-fin)*: Couldn't decide if it was better to be a lion or an eagle, so decided to be both.

**Hippocamps** *(HIPPO-camps)*: Part horse, part fish. A sort of sea-horse, if you like.

**Hydra** *(HY-druh)*: Nine-headed water monster. Hera somehow finds this loveable.

**Ladon** *(LAY-dun)*: A many-headed dragon that never sleeps (maybe the heads take turns?)

**Minotaur** *(MIN-uh-tor)*: A monster-man with the head of a bull. Likes eating people.

**Nemean Lion** *(NEE-mee-un)*: A giant, indestructible lion. Swords and arrows bounce off his fur.

**Pegasi** *(PEG-a-sigh)*: Mini flying horses with cute gold horns.

**Stymphalian Birds** *(stim-FAY-lee-un)*: Man-eating birds with metal feathers, metal beaks and toxic dung.

**Telchines** *(TELL-keens)*: Underwater monsters with dog heads and seal flippers. Scary.

## GODS AND GODDESSES:

**Amphitrite** *(AM-fih-TRY-tee)*: Sea Goddess and Poseidon's wife.

**Aphrodite** *(AF-ruh-DY-tee)*: Goddess of Love and Beauty and all things pink and fluffy.

**Ares** *(AIR-eez)*: God of War. Loves any excuse to pick a fight.

**Athena** *(a-THEE-na)*: Goddess of Wisdom and defender of pesky, troublesome Heroes.

**Artemis** *(AR-te-miss)*: Goddess of the Hunt. Can't decide if she wants to protect animals or kill them.

**Dionysus** *(DY-uh-NY-suss)*: God of Wine. Turns even sensible gods into silly goons.

**Eos** *(EE-oss)*: Goddess of the Dawn. Fond of pink.

**Hades** *(HAY-deez)*: Zeus's youngest brother and the gloomy Ruler of the Underworld.

**Helios** *(HEE-lee-us)*: The bright, shiny and blinding God of the Sun.

**Hephaestus** *(Hih-FESS-tuss)*: God of Blacksmithing, Metal, Fire, Volcanoes, and everything awesome.

**Hera** *(HEER-a)*: Zeus's scary wife. Drives a chariot pulled by screechy peacocks.

**Hermes** (HER-MEEZ): Michievous Messenger God with a handy invisibility hat and winged sandals.

**Hestia** *(HESS-tee-ah)*: Goddess of the Hearth and Home. Bakes the most heavenly treats.

**Persephone** *(per-SEF-oh-nee)*: Goddess of Spring, stolen away by Hades to be his wife. Made bad mistake of eating pomegranate seeds in the Underworld.

**Poseidon** *(puh-SY-dun)*: God of the Sea and controller of supernatural events.

**Zeus** *(ZOOSS)*: King of the Gods. Fond of smiting people with lightning bolts.

## OTHER MYTHICAL BEINGS:

**Arachne** *(ar-AKK-nee)*: Brilliant weaver. Turned into a spider by Athena for boasting about her skill. Oops.

**Autolycus** *(AW-toe-lie-CUSS)*: A very naughty boy. Stole some cattle and blamed it on Heracles.

**Cherubs** *(CHAIR-ubs)*: Small flying babies. Mostly cute.

**Dryads** *(DRY-ads)*: Tree spirits. Only slightly more serious than nymphs.

**Epimetheus** *(ep-ee-MEE-thee-us)*: Prometheus's silly brother who designed animals. Thank him for giving us the platypus and naked mole rat.

**Eurydice** *(YOUR-id-ee-see)*: Tree-nymph and all-time

greatest love of Orpheus. Stepped on a snake by mistake. Died.

**Geryon** *(JAYR-ee-un)*: A cattle-loving giant with a two-headed dog.

**Heracles** *(HAIR-a-kleez)*: The half-god 'hero' who was given twelve impossible tasks by scary Hera, including stealing poor Cerberus from the Underworld and dragging him up to Earth. Loooves killing magical beasts.

**Lethe** *(LEE-thee)*: Memory-stealing spirit of forgetfulness. Lives in a marsh.

**Maenads** *(MAY-nads)*: Followers of Dionysus, lovers of dancing and partying.

**Naiads** *(NYE-ads):* Water spirits. Keeping Olympus clean and refreshed since 500 BC.

**Nerieds** *(NEAR-ee-ids)*: Sea nymphs. Daughters of Nereus, the Old Man of the Sea.

**Nereus** *(NEH-re-us)*: The Old Man of the Sea, a shapeshifter fond of wrestling heroes like Heracles.

**Nymphs** *(NIMFS)*: Giggly, girly, dancing nature spirits.

**Orion** *(oh-RY-on)*: Starry hunter killed by a scorpion.

**Orpheus** *(or-FEE-us)*: Magnificent musician who tried to rescue his beloved Eurydice from the Underworld. (Massive fail there, then.)

**Pandora** *(pan-DOR-ah)*: The first human woman. Accidentally opened a jar full of evil.

**Prometheus** *(pruh-MEE-thee-us)*: Gave fire to mankind, and was sentenced to eternal torture by bird-pecking.

**Satyrs** *(SAY-ters)*: 50% goat, 50% human. 100% party animal.

**Silenus** *(sy-LEE-nus)*: Dionysus's best friend. Old and wise, but not that good at beast-care.

**Tritons** *(TRY-tuns)*: Half man, half two-tailed fish.

# PLACES:

**Arcadia** *(ar-CAY-dee-a)*: Wooded hills in Greece where the nymphs and dryads like to play.

**Macris** (MACK-riss): Large seahorse-shaped island off the Greek coast where Poseidon has his second palace.

**Tartarus** *(TAR-ta-russ)*: A delightful torture dungeon miles below the Underworld.

**The Underworld**: Hades' happy little kingdom of dead people, also known as Hell in Northern parts.